THE WAY TO MAKE PERFECT MOUNTAINS

Native American Legends of Sacred Mountains as told by Byrd Baylor

Illustrations by Leonard F. Chana

Cinco Puntos Press

El Paso, Texas

Library of Congress Cataloging-in-Publication Data

Baylor, Byrd.
       [God on every mountain top]
       The way to make perfect mountains: Native American legends
    of sacred mountains /as told by Byrd Baylor.
              p.   cm.
       Originally published: God on every mountain top. New York:
    Scribner, 1981.
       Includes bibliographical references.
       Summary: Presents a collection of legends about North American
    Indians.
        ISBN 0-938317-26-1
       1. Indians of North America—Folklore.   [1. Indians of North
    America—Southwest, New—Folklore.]   I. Title.
    E98.F6B36   1997
    398.2'08997—dc21
                                                        96-40531
                                                          CIP
                                                          AC

Book design by Geronimo Garcia of El Paso, Texas.

CONTENTS

In the north, a black mountain standing,
In the east, a white mountain standing,
In the south, a blue mountain standing,
In the west, a yellow mountain standing.

And a god is standing on each mountain top.

—*from the Navajo Mountain chant*

There Are Certain Mountains
Indians Know Are Holy Places

You can tell which ones they are
because storm clouds gather at their peaks
and lightning strikes more often
than it does on other mountains
and eagles circle in the afternoons
and winds *begin* up there.

Those are the mountains
where the power of ancient spirits
still hovers like a mist.
Those are the mountains
where gods still live and plant their corn
and dance.

In the southwest, each tribe has a homeland
marked off by sacred mountains
and each mountain has a story.

Call them myths — or call them truth.
It doesn't matter.

Just remember that people who have looked
at sacred mountains all their lives
say nothing is as real
as the high thin music they have heard
coming from inside the rocks up there.

What is written here is what the people tell
about their mountains.

These are stories from a time
when the world was new — and softer —
and magic was much better understood
than it is now.

To tell them is to honor
sacred mountains.

BEGINNINGS

How the Tewa Came to Sacred Mountains

They lived down below this world
in another world that was under a lake,
and gods lived with them there,
and animals and birds.
All of them spoke one language.
It was Tewa.

The world up here was a hazy, misty place,
still mud, too soft for people to walk on.

Down below, the people waited
for this world to harden.

When that time came,
they sent four pairs of messengers
up through the lake to scout around
and see what it was like.
And right away, they saw four great mountains
holding up the sky,
four great sacred mountains shining
in the four directions,
marking the boundaries of that world.

The mountain to the north was turquoise blue,
to the west, yellow,
to the south, red,
and to the sunrise it was white.

Other mountains marked the fifth direction — up,
and the sixth direction — down,
and the center of the world —
exactly where the people stood.

There was already monsters here
and Evil Beings in shadowy places
and giants in caves,
but a pair of gods went up to live
on each one of those mountains
so the people knew
they would be safe.

They said it was the world they wanted.

A Sacred Mountain for Mohaves

Two gods leaned down against the earth
and heard faint, far-off murmurings underground.

They knew it was the sound of people, stirring.
They knew they must be getting restless,
moving closer to the top.

So they said, "Let's help them up."

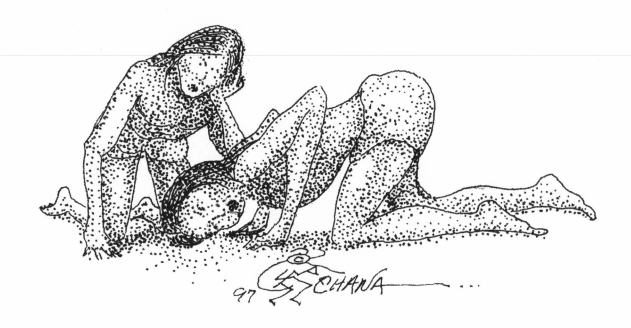

They found the softest place there was
and pushed long thin willow poles in there,
and down inside, the people saw that speck of light.

That's where they came climbing up —
near the place of Needles Mountain.

People gathered there in groups.
The two gods told each tribe
which way to walk to find a home.
They sent them off in each direction.
but they said to the Mohaves,
"You stay here. You'll be happy in this sacred spot
beside a sacred mountain."

And it was true. They are still happy there.

The Way to Make Perfect Mountains

When the Dineh — the Navajo people — came into this world
they saw no mountains here.

They had come climbing through a reed,
up from the world below.
Down there, they had their sacred mountains
and they wanted mountains here.

First Man told the people,
"I have brought them with me."

And it was true because he had some sand
from each one of those mountains
wrapped up in his medicine bag.
From that, First Man and First Woman
said they could start new mountains.

To make the Mountain of the East
they mixed sand from below with white shell
and fastened mountain to earth
with a zig-zag lightning flash.
The Navajo color for East is white
so they put white pigeon eggs on the summit
of the new East Mountain.
(Wild pigeons fly there now.)

The Mountain of the South was made
with sand and blue-green turquoise
and fastened with a great flint knife
shaped like the point of an arrow.
The color for South is blue
so they gave South Mountain bluebird eggs.
(Bluebirds fly there now.)

The Mountain of the West was made
with yellow-red sand and abalone shell
and fastened with a sunbeam.
Yellow is the color for West
so they gave West Mountain the eggs of the yellow warbler.
(Yellow warblers fly there now.)

The Mountain of the North was made
with black sand and jet
and fastened with a rainbow.
Black is the color for North
so they gave North Mountain blackbird eggs.
(Blackbirds fly there now.)

They put perfect plants and animals up there,
perfect rain and perfect mist.

Songs and chants were made for every mountain.
They have not changed since then.
(You hear them now.)

When an Eagle Led the People

The Taos people came up from a lake
far to the north.

Then they wandered,
walking, searching, always looking
for the center of the world,
for the place where they would stay.

As they walked, they saw an eagle
circling high above them
and they said,
"That eagle knows the way."

He stayed with them
and led them south.
One day he soared above a mountain
that held a blue lake in its peak.

"Build two pueblos now,"
the eagle called out in their language.

Then he flew straight into the sun
while down below
the people made their promises
to stay by Taos Mountain.

The Way to Stretch a Mountain

Jicarilla Apaches came to this world
through a hole in a mountain
and they built that mountain themselves.

They took handfuls of colored sand,
black, blue, yellow, and glistening,
and made small mountains
shaped like tipis
and placed them carefully in a row
from east to west.
On each one they put the seeds
of all the things they liked to eat
and the needles and leaves of their favorite trees.
On top they stuck a reed
and tied a downy feather there
and gave it pure water to make it grow.

Birds and animals used their power.
People used their power, singing.

The four small mounds of sand
began to grow into one gleaming mountain.
It grew in jumps, four times.
Each time it moved there was a noise.

Looking up, the people saw
the berries and the yucca fruit
and the streams of water
and the cottonwoods and aspens
and the ripe wild cherries.

But then two people slipped away
and went running up the mountainside
laughing and shouting and gathering cherries.
They stepped on the new tender grasses,
forgetting to honor the mountain.

The mountain stopped growing.

Wind went to find out what was wrong
and brought those two back down.
In shame and sorrow, every creature
begged the mountain please
to grow again.

And four times more,
it grew
but it would not grow tall enough
to reach the other world.

So Spider made a web up to the sun
and pulled four sun rays down —
one black, one blue, one yellow, one glistening.
She tied them to the four sides of the mountain
and tugged until that mountain stretched
up to this world.

The people came out
exactly in its center.

They came out happy
from Big Mountain.

CHANGES

Ceremony for Moving Mountains

Elder Brother gave the Tohono O'odham a desert world
and marked it off with mountains.

But there was one thing wrong.

The mountains stood so close together
that the valley in the center
was not large enough for all the fields
of beans and wheat and squash and corn
the people wanted.

They said, "It would be good if we could
just push those mountains back."

Four medicine men climbed up the steep rock cliffs
of Baboquivari Mountain.
All day they sat with their strong thoughts.

When they came down, they told the people what to do
and it was this:
Prepare a great summer feast with saguaro fruit wine.
Make a ceremony that will move the mountains back.

The people gathered ripe red sweet saguaro cactus fruit.
They lit the fires at sunrise and cooked the fruit all day.
They took it off the fire at sunset.
They put it into ollas and waited there four days
before the feast was ready.

Then the people danced. Nobody slept at all.
They sang the oldest kind of earth songs.
They sat in rows facing the mountains they wanted to move.

At the end of the first day
the mountains did not look quite so hard.

At the end of the second day
you could see the mountains quiver.

At the end of the third day
the mountains were slowly, slowly, beginning to move.

The people sang harder, danced harder.
They feasted all through the night.

At the end of the fourth day, as the sun went down bright red,
the mountains shook so wildly that the top of Baboquivari
broke away and fell. The peak rolled down.

The mountains moved back to the place where they are now.

When Four Winds Moved Four Mountains

The new world was so small
that when the sun first crossed the sky
it did not have far to go.
It came close to the earth,
drying up corn plants,
scorching the hogans,
burning the Navajo people.

They covered their eyes
from the blinding light.
They tried to hide
from the heat.

"We cannot live in such a world,"
they said.

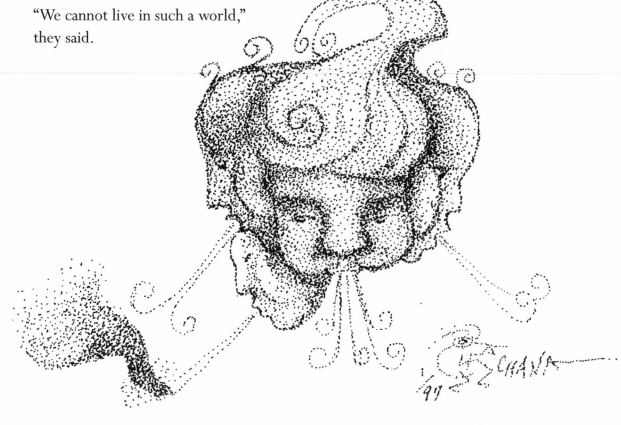

They called the four Winds
and each one came down from his mountain
into that hot dry world.

"Use your strength," the people said.
"If you could pull your mountains back
there would be a larger space
for the sun to move across."

So with all their strength
the four Winds pushed against
the four great mountains.
Howling and gusty and loud and wild
they blew all day.

The second day the mountains moved
but the sun was still too close.
Again the people asked for help.
Again the four Winds blew.

The third day was better.

The fourth day was fine.
The people said, "This is the way we want it."

The Flood

Water covered every cactus
and mesquite and palo verde tree
in the Pima's desert world.

Earth Doctor told the people
to take their cooking ollas
and baskets full of seeds and grain
and climb up on Crooked Peak
in the Superstition Mountains.

But even there the water rose.
It lapped at their feet.

"If the mountain could grow
we would be saved," they said.

Earth Doctor sang four times.
Each time his magic song was heard
the mountain grew.
But each time, the water rose again.

After the fourth song
the mountain stopped growing.

There was only one thing more
that Earth Doctor could do.
He chanted these words:
"Powerless ... powerless.
Powerless is my magic crystal.
My people shall become as stone."

He hit the mountainside with his right hand
and thunder roared in all directions.
At that second, the people turned to stone.

They are rocks up on the mountain now.
You see them as they were,
some bending down over their ollas,
beginning to cook,
some standing close together, talking,
some with their carrying baskets
looking out over the dark stormy world.

You can still see the ridge of foam
where the water stopped
at the very top of those people-rocks.

PROTECTION

Mountain Against Mountain

When people were at war
their mountains tried to help them.

Sierra Estrella was a mountain
that loved all Maricopas.
Four peaks was one that loved all Yavapais.

The tribes along the Gila River used to watch
those mountains fight.
They heard them argue and debate.

When their tribes were at war,
the mountains shouted threats across the desert.
Sometimes their anger was so great
they fought all through the day.
People far away could see the blowing sand
and hear the thunder and the falling rocks.

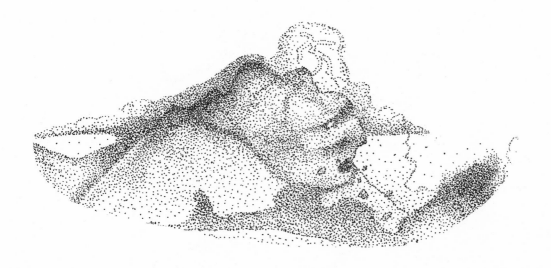

When Four Peaks won, the Yavapai were strong.
If Four Peaks lost, they always had bad luck.

And when Estrella won, it sang and danced
and every Maricopa felt that joy.
If they went into battle then, they won.

When Estrella lost, it sat and mourned,
pulling the darkness around it,
sad that its people would suffer.

The power of a mountain was so strong
that if one man killed another in a battle
he would quickly turn away
from that man's sacred mountain
before the mountain saw his face.

Nobody wanted a mountain to hate him.

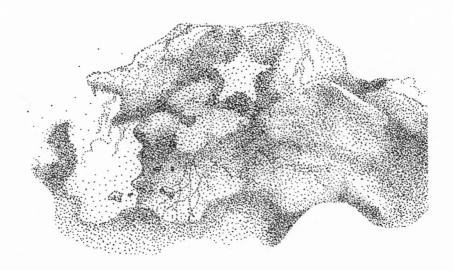

How Mountains Saved
the Tohono O'odham

The crops were ripe,
ready to harvest.
The Desert People were in their fields.

From behind a mountain
their enemies came running,
wanting to take
all their beans and their grain.

Up and down the mountainside
the people fought.
The mountain knew
the Desert People were losing
so it did what it could.
It opened holes in the rocky cliffs
to let its friends see through.
(Those holes are there today.)

Then it called to its stronger brother,
Baboquivari, the sacred mountain
of that tribe.

Across the desert,
Baboquivari heard that call.

He sent Wind Man and Cloud Man
down to the battle.

Cloud Man made cradles out of
soft summer clouds.
Wind Man lifted up the children
and put them in the cradles
and sailed them through the sky
to Baboquivari Mountain
where they would be safe.

Then heavy black storm clouds
went down to the battle.
They covered the people.
No one could see.
In that darkness,
Wind Man lifted up his warrior friends
and took them back with him
to Baboquivari
wrapped in clouds.

Clouds hover near that mountain
even now.

When Mountains Could Open and Close

No mountains ever loved a tribe
more than Apache mountains loved Apache people.

When someone was in danger
he would run straight to a mountain
and a sheer rock wall would open
wide enough to let him in.
Then it would close.

Safe inside the mountain,
he would hear the enemy ride by,
would even hear them saying,
"That man just disappeared!"

Sometimes, while he was waiting there,
the Mountain Spirits would dance for him
and let him learn their songs
and see their masks.

Once, on the plains at the foot
of the Chuchillo Mountains,
Apaches fought with bows and arrows
against men who fought with guns.

Wind saw the battle
and hurried on to tell the mountains that
Apaches were in trouble.

Then, shouting and calling
and waving their long painted swords,
Mountain Spirits rushed out of the mountain.

They surrounded the enemy horsemen.
Suddenly, there at the foot of the mountain,
a cave appeared
where only rocks had been before.

The enemy rode in.
The mountain quickly closed
and held them there
just long enough to let
all the Apaches ride away.

When they looked back,
the Mountain Spirits had disappeared.

There wasn't anything to see
on all that plain
but a small band of Apaches
going home.

POWER, MAGIC, MYSTERY, AND DREAMS

Magical Birth on a Mountain Top

For four days, a dark mysterious cloud
was seen above the central sacred mountain
of the Navajo world.

At the end of four days,
it wrapped itself around the mountain top
and rain fell there,
a sign that something wonderful
was taking place.

First Man went up there
singing a Blessing song.

Where the cloud had been,
he found a sleeping baby.

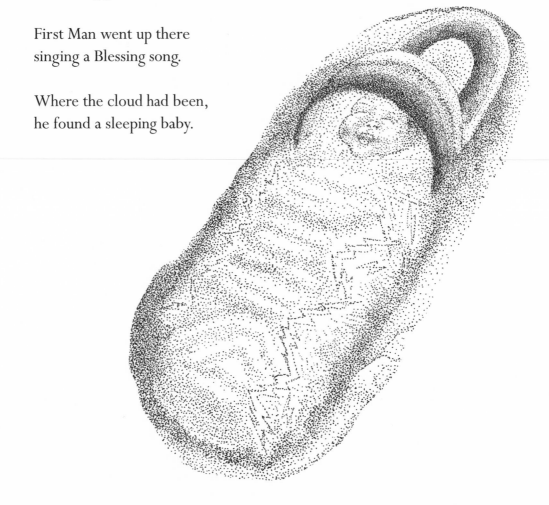

The cradle that held her
was made of two short curving rainbows
with red sunrays crossing
at the baby's feet and chest.
Another rainbow arched over her face.

Inside the cradle she was wrapped
in blankets of soft, colored clouds.
The lacing that held the clouds in place
was made of zigzag lightning
and of sunbeams.

First Man took the baby down the mountain.
First Woman fed her pollen
and broth and the dew of flowers.

Because her name was Changing Woman,
Turquoise Woman,
she grew up faster than human children do.
In two days, she sat up, smiling.
In four days, she walked.

Later she had five hogans
where she lived on Whirling Mountain.
Her hogans are still there.
You can see where they have turned to stone.

Touching a Mountain's Power

Suppose a Yuma man had special power.
Suppose he dreamed of eagles.

He might be lifted up
to the mountain tops
and moved along a road of spiderweb
that runs from peak to peak
connecting every sacred butte and mountain.

In a dream, he was usually led by a bird
on that spiderweb trail.
In a single night he went
hundreds of miles.
At the top of each mountain
the spirit of the mountain
taught him its special song,
its special kind of curing,
and its power.

In those days, the tribes along the Gila River
used to hear their healers tell
of going all the way
from Tempe Butte
to the San Francisco Mountains—
looking down on Rainbow Bridge—
and far across the desert back to
Awikwame, the Mohave's sacred mountain.

One who knew the secrets of those mountain peaks
knew *everything*.

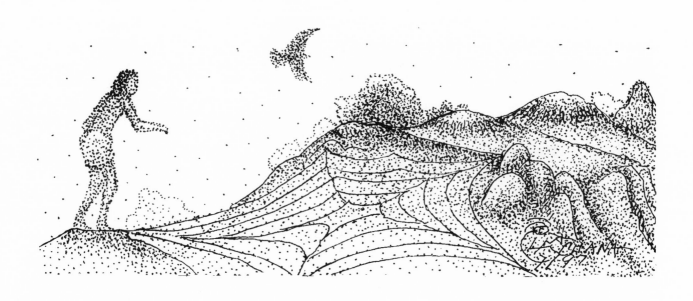

From Sandia Mountain to Sky Pueblo

Up on Sandia Mountain
Spider Woman has her home.

Once long ago a man
from Sandia Pueblo
climbed up there to ask
for Spider Woman's help.

He said his wife
had been stolen away
and taken to a pueblo in the sky
where he could never go.

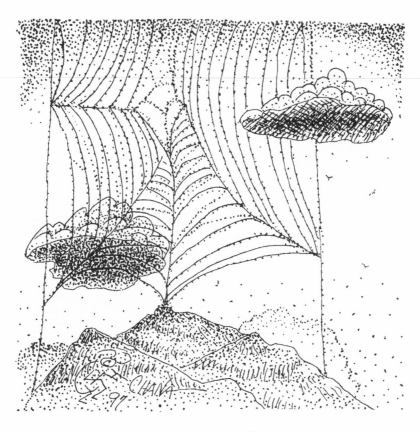

Spider Woman spun a web
that reached from the mountain
straight up through the stars
to Sky Pueblo.
Hidden by darkness,
they traveled along
that gleaming spiderweb bridge.

The man found his wife
and they hurried back over the web
to the mountain
and down to their home
in the valley.

When Spider Woman pulled her web
out of the sky
there was no way for anyone up there
to guess how they had come … or gone.

How the Zunis Were Welcomed at the Rainbow Cave

The Zunis used to look up at Corn Mountain
and see orange and pink and violet mists
rising from the Cave of the Rainbows.

They noticed that flute music
drifted down to them
whenever those mists were seen.

On one of those days
all the Zuni War Priests
walked up the mountain trail
following the music
and the pale green mist
to the place where Sun Youth lives
inside his Rainbow Cave.

As they stood at the entrance
the flute song stopped.
Suddenly, each man was wrapped
in hazy, many-colored rainbow mist.

With those clouds around them,
they went inside the cave
and found that all the spirits of that place
were waiting to greet them.

They were beautiful, the Zunis said.
And each one held a long, thin,
brightly painted flute.
They handed four flutes
to the War Priests.

Now at winter solstice time
the Zunis too play flutes
while going up Corn Mountain
to leave their offerings.

How the Maricopas
Made Wishes Come True

They used to climb to a windy cave
up in the Painted Rock Mountains.

It was a place where any wish
was granted.

You had to go alone.
You had to creep
through a small dark hole
and sit there facing the light.
You had to hold your right hand out
and think of what you wanted.

It could be anything—
good crops or turquoise
or luck in racing
or someone to love.

But first, you had to sit there
in the dark.
Behind you, you would hear
a Whirlwind Person
roaring through the mountain,
coming closer,
wrapping its loud winds
around you.
And you'd feel something *cold*
in your outstretched hand.

If you ran away in fear,
bad luck would follow you forever.
But if you stayed
and weren't afraid
and closed your hand slowly
over that *cold,*
and fasted four days—

you'd have your wish.

How the Yaquis Made Wishes Come True

Any talent you could ever want
is in a mountain called Sikil Kawi.

The only way to enter
is to push yourself between the rocks
into a hole no larger than
a small fox den.

Inch by inch, you twist and squirm
through a passage that leads to a cave.

You sit down on a log to rest
but the log turns into a snake
and wraps itself around you.
Wherever you look,
wild animals move in the shadows.

But if you show no fear at all,
an old man leads you to the place
where all the magic talents
are hanging on a wall
and you can take the one you want.

Maybe you choose the *harp* or the *drum*
or *riding horseback* or *carving masks*
or *knowing how to make yourself invisible.*

When you leave, you walk by rattlesnakes.
At that moment, if you are afraid,
your fear will change you
into one of those animals
you saw in the cave.

But if you get back to the world again,
you'll be the best at whatever you do.

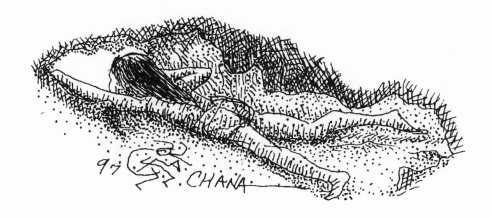

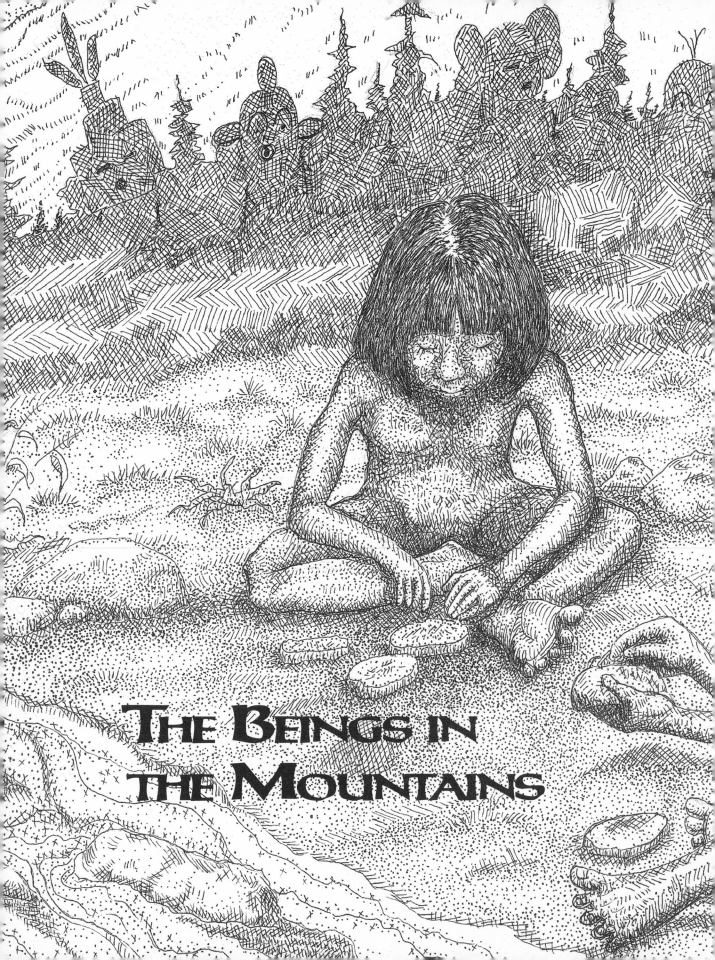

THE BEINGS IN THE MOUNTAINS

Where Kachinas Live

Hidden in a perfect world
inside the San Francisco Peaks,
Kachinas live.

Everything they want is there …
corn and squash and beans of every kind,
all the wild plants that are good to eat,
all the rabbit brush and yucca that they need
for making baskets.

They have lakes and springs where cattails grow.
They have all the sacred trees:
blue spruce, mountain mahogany, piñon, and juniper.

When they want rain, they call dark clouds.
When they want songs, they send for birds.

In ancient times,
Kachinas lived up on the mesas
with the Hopi people all year long.

Now they only live there half the year
when people need Kachinas most
to dance for them
and bless the growing crops
and bring the rain.

Then they disappear, walking off across the mesa,
westward to the sunset,
going where the rain clouds are,
back to their perfect world.

Certain Hopis, taking offerings
to that high mountain place,
have heard the singing and the drums
inside the sacred peaks.
And they have seen where children
from the Kachinas' hidden world
make mud pies by the streams
and leave their tiny handprints on the rocks.

A Safe Home for Iitoi

A cave on the rocky side
of Baboquivari Mountain
marks the center of the world
for the Tohono O'odham Nation.
It marks the entrance
to the hidden home of Iitoi.

Not far away, worn deep into the rock,
you see the grinding holes
where he used to grind
his mesquite beans.

On the north side of the mountain,
he kept his grinding stone, his good metate.
On the south side,
he kept two racing balls.
When he was somewhere down below,
all he had to do was sing a special song
and Wind would come along
and carry him up there again.

When he went away, he always left
his woven sleeping mat rolled up.
Its mark is there today,
in rock.

When the Desert People needed him
to kill one of the monsters
that roamed the early world
they went up there to ask for help
from Iitoi, their Elder Brother.

They always found
an old bent-over man,
hardly able to move.
But when he came down the mountain
he was young and powerful again.

In ancient days, when Iitoi had many enemies,
he built his home inside that mountain.
Circling it in all directions,
he made a maze of dark narrow
underground tunnels.
No enemy was ever able to find his way
into the safe quiet peaceful center
where Elder Brother lived.

Now the Desert People all feel safe
when they can see that mountain.

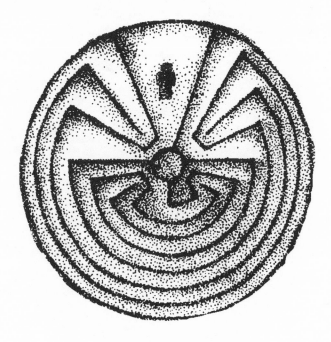

Where the Little Twin War Gods Used to Play

Rising high above the plains of Zuni
are the sheer steep cliffs of Towayalane,
the great Corn Mountain.

This is where the Twin War Gods
ran up and down laughing and joking
and driving their grandmother crazy
with their dangerous tricks.

With small rainbows for their bows,
thunderbolts for arrows,
swift lightning shafts
pointed with turquoise,
those two were the
Slayers of Monsters.
Every day they thought of some new way
of getting rid of cannibal giants
and ogres and whippers
and witches and anything bad.

The Zuni people used to hear them
laughing as they ran,
used to see them traveling
across the bright blue sky on rainbows.

Now the spirit of the younger twin
watches over Zuni from his shrine
on Towayalane
while the elder twin looks down
from his place up on Twin Mountain.

They don't have any monsters left to kill
but they still see that the Zunis are safe.

A World for Mountain Spirits

The Mountain Spirits
that they call the Gan
need mountains as wild
and strong and free and beautiful
as *they* are.

They have those mountains
in Apacheland.

There was a time
when Mountain Spirits
lived in the world of people
but they wanted a place
without Sickness or Death
so they would live forever.

Hummingbird knew of a world
like that.
He told them where to find it
inside Apache mountains.

But before they left,
the Mountain Spirits
chose the people
who would take their place.
They gave them masks and songs
and all the ceremonies they would need
to make life good
and keep Apaches strong.

The Gan still live
inside the cliffs and caves
in the world where nobody dies.
When Apaches need them, they are there.

In times of trouble,
people say a mountain cliff
has opened wide enough
to let Apaches come inside
and touch the power of the Gan
and take their blessings back
to all the others.

And there is a certain narrow canyon
that Apaches know.
At a certain time of day,
if they put their ears against
its rocky wall,
they hear the far faint drumming
and the singing
and the strange mysterious call
that Mountain Spirits make.

They know they can't be far away.

The Stories Here

The stories here
are just a few
of the ones we like to think about
when we look at sacred mountains.

Each mountain has a hundred more.

In the southwest, people know
to walk on sacred mountains
gently.

And they know that some
are not to be walked on
at all
except by people of that tribe
and even then
only with offerings
at special times.

People who have looked
at sacred mountains all their lives
say you always find one mountain
that you can't forget.

Even when you're somewhere far away
you'll suddenly remember
the color of those rocks
and how the light shines there
and you'll know
that's where you ought to be
because in some strange way
that mountain is your home.

May your path lead you there …

At the edge of the mountain
A cloud hangs.
And there my heart, my heart, my heart
Hangs with it.

— from the Tohono O'odham

Author's note:

These tales go back to the beginning of tribal memory, but they are a part of the present, too. In the southwest, several tribes are fighting legal battles even now for control of their own shrines and sacred mountains, trying (usually with little success) to keep mines and ski lodges and land developers away from the homes of their gods.

There are dozens of versions of each story included here, and there are other stories not included because they were too private to tell outside one tribe. I probably began this book (without knowing it) years ago when an O'odham friend told me she felt safe wherever she could see Baboquivari Mountain. Now I too live where I see Baboquivari and I too feel safe.

In collecting these stories, I looked for the oldest sources and best translations and compared them with what people in different tribes had already told me. Then I looked at the mountains a long time…

Here are some of the books I read. They go back almost a hundred years to the early ethnologists who recognized the importance of southwestern Indian culture, and they include new publications by the tribes themselves.

Long Ago Told: Papago Indian Legends, by Harold Bell Wright. D. Appleton & Co., 1929.

Myths and Tales of the Chiricahua Apache Indians, by Morris Opler. American Folklore Society Memoirs, volume 37, 1942.

Navajo Legends, translated by Washington Matthews. American Folklore Society, 1897.

Navajo Religion, by Gladys A. Reichard. Pantheon Books, 1950.

Outlines of Zuni Creation Myths, by Frank H. Cushing.
U.S. Bureau of American Ethnology, 13th annual report, 1891.

Pajarito Plateau and Its Ancient Peoples, by Edgar Lee Hewett.
University of New Mexico Press and School of American
Research, 1938.

Papago Indian Religion, by Ruth M. Underhill. Columbia
University Press, 1946.

Pueblo Gods and Myths, by Hamilton A. Tyler. University of
Oklahoma Press, 1964.

The Sacred —Ways of Knowledge, Sources of Life, by Peggy V. Beck
and A.L. Walters. Navajo Community College, Tsaile, Ariz.,
Navajo Nation, 1977.

The Tewa World: Space, Time and Being, by Alfonso Ortiz.
University of Chicago Press, 1969.

Yoeme: Lore of the Arizona Yaqui People, by Mini Valenzuela
Kaczkurkin. English Department, University of Arizona.

Yuma Tribes of the Gila River, by Leslie Spier. University of
Chicago Press, 1933.

Zuni Mythology, by Ruth Benedict. Columbia University
Contributions to Anthropology #21, 1935.

The Zuni People — Self Portraits by the Zuni People, translated by
Alvina Quam. University of New Mexico Press, 1972.

BYRD BAYLOR

Byrd Baylor has always lived in the Southwest, mainly in Southern Arizona near the Mexican border. She is at home with the southwestern desert cliffs and mesas, rocks and open skies. She is comforted by desert storms. The Tohono O'odham people are her neighbors and close friends.

Byrd has written many books for children. She is well known for such favorites as *Amigo, When Clay Sings* and *The Way to Start A Day*. Her books have been honored with many prestigious children's book awards, including the Caldecott Award. All of her books are full of the places and the peoples that she knows. She thinks of these books as her own kind of private love songs to the place she calls home.

LEONARD F. CHANA

Leonard F. Chana was born in the fall of 1950 into the Kaij Mek (Burnt Seed) community, now called Santa Rosa Village, in the heart of the Tohono O'odham Nation.

In the 1970's, Leonard began to pursue his interest in making art. He developed his own personal style of stippling—images are formed with dots in pen and ink—for expressing Tohono O'odham life and traditions. Leonard says of his art, "My first art was drawings of my pride in being Indian. I drew Indians with feathers, teepees…the Hollywood Indian. But I felt something missing in my heart—the same feeling I got coming home from boarding school after five years. Memories of a comfortable time when all the elders were there, and the magic (culture and tradition) that kept us alive, swirled through and around us. Now the elders are gone and there are few left to teach but bits and pieces of the O'odham *hindag* (the way of the people)."

Leonard lives in Tucson with his wife Barbara and their family.